WHAT

LIES

AHEAD?

WHAT LIES AHEAD?

Truly,

Shanny

Published by Truly Omi,

ISBN-13: 978-0-692-86036-6

ISBN-10: 0-692-86036

Author: Shanny Samuels

Publisher: Truly Omi, Shanny Samuels

Editors: Rochelle Hampton, Shahna Currie

Cover: Quan and Derron

Music Quotes: "Dope Bitch and Trap Queen"

-Nisha Blanco with permission from Nisha Blanco follow On S.M. @Nishv Blvnco
Printing company: @tpfimprints

"Wake Me Up" -3D Na'tee with permission from 3D Na'tee Follow on S.M. @3dnatee & 3dnatee.com

Author's Note

This book came about at a very crazy and confusing time
in my life. Outside of music it was the one thing that kept
me sane. I've always been good at storytelling and I have
always loved to write. I went and bought two notebooks,
one I formed this masterpiece and the other I strategized.
There were rough days and days I didn't write at all but I
stayed focused and consistent. If you know me, you know
there is always multiple meanings for everything I do. The
main thing I want my readers to take from this is how
lying and keeping secrets are one in the same and the
damage that could come from it could cost you
everything. It has been a long process but I got it done.
First and foremost, I'd like to Thank Myself! We did it!
And My City! Detroit for making me ME!
I had help along this journey and I'd like to thank all those
who helped bring this together.
My mentor Mrs. Currie, I couldn't Thank you enough well
until these m's roll in.
My sister Chellie, There's No Shanny without Chellie
Know Dat! ~Loyalty is Law! And The person who was
pressed and heard my mouth the most my best friend
Quan! Words could never. oh yea and I guess Derron (lol)
just joking thank you for everything. This was impossible
without yall so again Thanks For dealing with my
craziness and demands and making this possible. My sister
Kema, who was on the phone through majority of this

process hearing me rant and stress out and just being you. I really appreciate yall! My siblings Tevin, Shaqil, Sid, PRINCESS, My Princess, Nevaeh, Skyler, and Summer. My Mother, I love you boo thank you isn't enough neither is banding words together to show gratitude. My favorites and the way stayed sane, Nisha Blanco & 3D Na'tee (there wasn't A day that passed I wasn't vibing to one or both of yall). Yall both already know how crazy I am about yall and yall music. I hold on to those words and push through it all. I love yall and Thanks to Everybody that love me and everybody who dont.

Prologue

Knock, Knock, Knock

Who is it? Who the fuck is it?

Knock, knock, knock,

What the fuck? I said who is it as the door is opened

Tiny? You ok?

     No bro I just need a shoulder and an ear walking inside the two-bedroom apartment and taking a seat at the dining room table, head still down and a face full of tears.

Bro? With a look of confusion

     Tell me you aint know about it? Never mind you not gone tell me.

Know what? what the fuck you talking about?

     Yo trifling ass friend fuckin that nasty bitch and raw too he gone catch something.

Yall been fighting again? Here I know you want this Passing a blunt.

That's yo friend he ain't called you yet? I tried to kill him and her!

Who? What happened?

Trying to fight back the tears! I just don't know bro. I deal with so much shit from him and I don't know if I can continue to.

What you done did now? And yall always go through this.

Just shut up and listen and you better stay mutual.

Do I ever take sides?

Always!

Anyways, I texted him earlier this morning and he was acting funny. Yall had a long practice, yesterday right? So, last night we aint talk but a few minutes after he made it home. It took him too long to respond in between text messages so I popped up. I guess he was too occupied with pussy in his mouth to hear me walk up the stairs.
When I opened the door to his room that bitch looked like a deer on a highway.

All I saw was dick, ass, and an iron. I grabbed the iron went upside his head a time or two he fell by his door. Then I slid across the bed like I was trying to steal home base and blacked out on her. I probably would've killed her if Twan didn't pick me up off her. She going to hospital for sure and he gone have a hell of A headache. Wiping tears from my face. (*Wow*)

Can I ask you a question? Have you cheated?

Nope! But I should've. I wanted this forever but I think it's time to explore more options.

Oh, really options huh? Flipping his lighter back and forth between his two fingers and the table.

This shit not fair! I swear I'm a great girlfriend he still doesn't act right what should I do?

Between me and you? Cheat back! Or leave him. That's the only way you gone feel better.

Lost in my own thoughts, the room grew quiet.
I wonder if he knows that I know? Interrupted.

Here spark this! And it looks like you could use this too.

Ooh yes Hennessy you know that's my favorite! Taking the glass to the head was a mistake but fuck it too late now.

I doubt it but imma play along.

If that nigga don't know what he got get a nigga that do.

None of you niggas do. So, what the fuck?

If it was me I wouldn't do that to you.

If it was you huh? That's your best friend yall do everything together. So, what would you do different?

No, we be together I'm my own man. And I know how to handle business.

Well handle it then.

Say no more.

Before I could react, his head was under my skirt and my pussy was in the back of his throat. Damn is all I could manage to say while pushing his head further and further in my ass. How was this so wrong but it felt so right? Getting closer and closer to climaxing the moans grew louder and louder and could be heard by anybody walking by. Moments before exploding, in walks his annoying ass brother. Luckily a wall was blocking his view and he went straight to his room.

Back to reality. Let me get out of here that was a close call.

Wait don't leave we got unfinished business.

I'm sorry we never should've, I gotta go. Dashing out the front door with mixed emotions I dialed up my bitch Ri she got to KNOW how both of these fuck niggas just tried it.

Damn nigga yo annoying ass had to come home didn't you? I told you that bitch wasn't loyal if you would've never walked in I would've fucked
Yeah whatever nigga knowing you, you probably slipped her a mickey or something.

Which Way Is Right?

August 14,2015 91 degrees 9:00 a.m.

The birds chirping, bees buzzing, the sun beaming down, with no wind in sight.

"But Tinyesha Marie Jones, I need you! Let's fix this." Could be heard coming through the speaker.

"NO FUCK YOU! IF YOU KEEP YO DICK IN YO PANTS, WE WOULDN'T HAVE TO FIX SHIT!" As Tiny abruptly ends the call, she tosses her phone in the passenger seat as she slams the door to her bright yellow Camaro. She speeds off and heads to her salon.

Tiny is the definition of a business woman and boy was she handling hers; a hair salon, barbershop and nail salon. She also owned several condominiums in the *Oath Estates* community. She'd only lease them out for 90 days' max; she figured just enough time to emerge from the dirt. Her usual tenants were around the way D boys coming to "get on".

Thoughts racing back and forth through her mind. *What the fuck wrong with this nigga? Do he think I'm stupid? But I can't leave him to dry like that. He fucked up this time.*

Oooh stupid ass! She shouts.

She reaches her salon pain, anxiety and anger clouded her judgment and her vision because she failed to see Rod Black Impala parked on side of the salon.

Jumping out, Tiny runs to her back office opens her safe, and removed an envelope. Dialing her best friend as she jumps back in her car and heads where she swore up and down she wasn't going. The phone rung 4 times before Sherri answered

Who you with? Where you at? Can you meet me? Tiny hits her with a million questions.

Where you at? Are you OK? Are you being followed?

"Bitch why the fuck you sound so got damn paranoid? Tiny snaps, what you doing you aint got no business? Or should I say who? "

You know me, well don't you?

The girls chuckle.

"Nah for real though I need you to come meet me. Tony called me sounding all weird talking about meet him and I got a weird feeling about it. You know we aint been talking since I caught him with the community pussy."

Damn. I need to know that yo head is clear Tee. I aint trying to bail you out.

"I'm good but why you aint left out yet? I need you I don't care who you fucking I am nervous RI."

OK. make sure you're not being followed and promise you not gone be mad at me!

"Girl you high? Paranoid ass. I should be the paranoid one. I don't know what the fuck is wrong with this nigga I catch him with this hoe now he thinks I'm supposed to just come running because he said so?"

RI laughs. Aint that what you doing though? But for real T. OK I promise!

Focused on the conversation Tiny never saw the black impala or Grey Taurus a few cars behind the impala make every turn and took every exit she did. She was off her game. She would've usually been picked up on it, but she was for sure being followed. The Grey Taurus saw the Camaro slowing down and decided to ride past.

The Impala, on the other hand, stopped and parked just perfect enough to see and not be seen. Tiny pulls up parks in a secluded area, takes a deep breath, and a few looks around. All she could see was trees.

Message to RI: **Bitch I got a funny feeling, get here quick.** Message sent.

Tony walks up and gets in the car. Were you followed?

Fuck you!

Tiny now isn't the time for this. Were you followed?

No dumb ass! What the fuck?

He snatches her phone and turns it off. "Get out of the car and shut the fuck up" as he grabs her by the hand.

Tony led her down this trail in the middle of what appeared to be some type of woods. Getting closer and closer

Tiny stops and asked: Are you trying to kill me, because its other ways we can settle this.

Tony looks at her with pain in his eyes: "Are you serious? You think I'd hurt you? That's so low of you.

This is what the fuck I've been doing. I wasn't fucking this bitch I been trying to figure out who her inside man was and I think I have a damn good idea. That hoe ass nigga Ron, supposed to be my fucking brother."

Hearing the pain in Tony voice and the sight of Sandy tied up and bloodied made Tiny both happy and sad.

It was like Déjà vu, except this was once again her reality. The exact same feeling that had come over her almost ten years ago, was also the same demon she fought on a day to day basis, Conflict. The same thing that turned her away from the streets was the same thing that secretively turned her on about them. The death of her parents.

Forever Changed

04/14/2005

Tinyesha Jones walks inside the gym to find Tony and hands him her keys.

Take my car to Ri's house when you get out of practice.

> Why? Where the fuck you going?

Squinting and annoyed. Home I got a migraine.

> Yea, alright. Why would I take yo car to Ri's house?

Because she taking me home and she gone spend the night tonight so she can bring my car with her.

> Don't make me fuck both y'all up.

Bye Antonius.

Sherri hits the unlock button. The two ride in complete silence till they reached Tiny's house.

I'll be back around five.

> Wait till six so you can get my car from Tony, alright.

Tinyesha walks in the house where she is met by her father.

Girl what yo ass doing here aren't you posed to be at school?

I got a migraine daddy I just wanna lay down.

Get you one of them aspirins out of the cabinet and lay down for a while I'll give you an hour. You know the rules.

Ok daddy. Can you get me some water?

Yep as he heads and grabs her a bottle water and the aspirins.

Thanks daddy as Tiny takes the pill.

Mhmm you know the rules baby girl?

Yes, I come home early I still got learning to do.

Life lessons baby girl life lessons.

Tinyesha walks up to her room. She starts shutting off all lights and sound then lays it down.

Thirty minutes later her Mom walks in. You OK baby?

Yes, mom I feel better now. Can u bring me the chess board? You know daddy gone make me play today.

Sure, sweetie as Tanya makes her way to her room and retrieves the chess board from the top of their closet. She hands it to Tiny. Need anything else sweetie?

No mom. Thanks. Just let daddy know I'm ready.

Ok baby.

Tanya heads to the back of the house standing in the door way shouting Eddie Ed!

What woman?

Yo daughter said she ready.

Alright tell her I'll be in there in a minute.

Back up the stairs, now standing in Tiny's doorway, Tinyesha he said he'll be up in a minute.

He in that shed doing God knows what! Where's your car?

Tony got it he's gonna drop it off at Ri's house later. She's staying over tonight.

Now you KNOW better!! That boy gone be riding around with some lil girl in yo car.

And Imma kill them both. Matter a fact, let me text him and let him know.

Tiny pulls her phone out and texts Tony just that: **If you have some lil bitch in my car Imma find out and kill both of y'all! K. Love you ttyl.**

Tanya laughs seeing a lot of herself in Tiny. Ok, now let me get back to my Family Feud I'm sure yo daddy will be in shortly. Tanya sitting on the couch enjoying her game shows as she did most days.

Tiny sits up on her bed and slid the chess board back, realizing it didn't have any pieces in it. She looks outside her bedroom window to shout to her daddy about the missing pieces but before she could get a word out two men ran from behind the shed. Ed had to know them because they weren't masked. Tiny instantly recognized the second one; her uncle G who was never much of an uncle.

Noooo!!! Tiny shouts, as she covers her mouth and hides under her bed startling Ed, Tanya, and the gunmen. Tanya jumped up and ran to the back door realizing her mistake a few seconds too late.

Ed turned around and shot his pistol twice catching the first person both times in his chest causing him to collapse. Stunned by the face of the second shooter stuttering g... G... G. he couldn't get a word out before.

Two bullets hit his temple and exposed his brains. Should've gave up the fuckin money. Now let me go finish off yo bitch.

Screaming, Tanya at a disadvantage leaving her pistol behind the pillow on the couch she began weeping at the door. Take it all, it's all in the shed. She spats. You Coward Motherfucka! How you kill yo own brother over money? Fuckin snake.

Shut up bitch! He smacks her across the face with his pistol.

Blood shot out her mouth. Pussy!

I'll show you a pussy

She spits at him. Remembering Tiny was home, she wanted to protect her. She lunged at G until they fell out the door and in the grass behind the house.

You never should've done that. Dumb bitch! He kicks her in the face sending her flying into the back of the house. And if that cunt you call yo daughter was home I'd kill her first and make you watch.

Tanya accepting her fate and feeling accomplished. She smirks. "See you in hell", were her last words before her brother-in-law blew her face off.

Tiny stayed under her bed helpless and scared to move.

The time went by like molasses, what seemed like hours passed before Tiny decided to come from under her bed. She grabs a backpack from her closet and begins stuffing it with miscellaneous items clothes, the chessboard and her mother's gun were few of the many items. Before heading out and walking six blocks to Sherri house. Noticing Sherri car wasn't home, Tiny let herself in through the back door and put her backpack in Sherri's closet. Trying to gather her thoughts she pulls her phone out and starts to scroll her contacts.

The Who? and The Now!

Tiny was far from your average chick. She obtained her Masters and opened her first business by the time she turned 21. Measuring 5'5" on a 32" 24" 39" frame. Soft chocolate skin and almond shaped eyes were just a taste of what complimented her body! Weighing in at 145lbs you would swear was mostly ass. Having a big round booty, flat stomach and perky breast all helped compliment her mental in a very deep and intriguing way. Tiny had it all. The total package beauty, the body and the brains. Not to mention, she had a perfect set of 32 to match her spirit. She was beautiful and bright. Getting to know Tiny personally would make anybody question how the hell she ended up with Tony.

Standing at 6'3 caramel, curly haired, fine brother! I failed to mention those long curly lashes and hazel eyes are why most people would consider him a pretty boy. That's why most people slept on his "loony" ways. Especially graduating from

WSU, with his Masters in health and science, Tony was everything but a pretty boy on the inside. From the outside looking in, Tony and Tiny was a match made in heaven. But from the flesh to the core, it was hell and demons parading. They complimented each other well physically, but mentally he was no match for her and emotionally he wasn't ready.

Tiny and Tony been together for ten years now. Each year they have a different issue and by issue, I mean woman or shall I say women. Each time she catches him cheating she threatens to leave and will fight any girl trying her boo. He so used to it now, he does it consistently with the comfort of knowing she'll always be there.

It's like the same song keeps playing over and over and over again. Tiny did her dirt too, but she'd never disrespect Tony or their relationship, ooh but on those break times she was getting hers in.

They've separated so many times throughout those ten years I've lost count.

Tony heads to the gym April 3, following his daily routine; stretching for two minutes, running the Treadmill for 20 minutes, 140lb squats, bench pressing maxing out at 325. Tony, or T, as his boys called him was 220 lbs. s]olid and packed a mean blow. While on the treadmill he puts on his music and raps along caught up in the music he finally noticed Sandy shaking her head laughing.

Sandy stands 5'4 yellow tone, straight up and down skin and bones. She never seems to get tired of those tired blonde lace fronts or those horrible blue contacts she swears are her natural eyes to add to the facade that she's foreign which seems to be popular these days.

Although she was lacking in the body department she makes up for it with her ability to move and groove and she put that to use; basic student in the day, basic stripper by night.

By basic you know that means beneath regular.

Everybody know she only go to school to collect them checks, that doesn't knock her hustle though, she still manages to maintain a B average. No matter her level of basic it didn't mean she couldn't or wouldn't succeed majoring in Basicology, better known as general education with a minor in home wrecking. It seems as if she put more effort in her minor than in her major.

Home-wrecker was her middle name. She had a rep for seducing other women men and refusing to let go. One time things got so bad, she spent two weeks in the county on harassment charges.

She was only granted bail because Joey decided not to go through with the case if she agreed to get counseling and remain distant. She did just that. They agreed having any sort of contact she would have to serve her two-year sentence for aggravated assault.

As Tony was walking off the treadmill Sandy lightly brush past his shoulders and gently slides her fingers across his abs. Sorry. She whispers, I didn't see you get off but I'm glad I bumped into you.

T mumbles. Me too.

She proceeds as provocatively as possible walking away without trying to seem too thirsty. As Tony walks away to the showers, bent over stretching Sandy watches his every move. Lusting after what is soon to become her boo. Tony had a rep for sleeping with every woman who had a name, many women around the city spoke on how good he laid his pipe not to mention his head game.

This caused Tiny to fight a lot of bitches, but that didn't stop Sandy from wanting a piece of the pie. She knew just how to do it, but if it was going to work, she had to act quickly she set the treadmill for ten minutes, calculating and praying for the "perfect" time to accidentally bump into her boo or so she claimed somewhere in that head space she called a brain.

She plugs her headphones into her phone and turns up her music. Rapping as she picks up her running speed, the timer reaches zero. She gets off the treadmill scanning the crowd making sure he hadn't snuck past and he hadn't. Little did she know he was waiting for her on the other side of the wall. Sandy accidentally walks into the Men's locker room; before she could turn around she's grabbed by her wrist and slammed against the wall. Now face to face, bodies in sync, lips so close they are sharing the same breath.

As T slides his fingers to her box and lightly kiss her neck. Sandy attempts to mumble something before T interrupts her: You knew where you were going, didn't you?

Sandy looks up into his eyes, I'm new here...

Stuttering. He smacks his lips, "Girl stop playing You want this dick, don't you?"

Biting her pointer finger she states, Yes I want it and I want it NOW. She starts reaching for his zipper. He slaps her hand down, dismissing the budge in his pants he pulls away and says, exactly that's why I won't do this, not here, not never.

That's what you think. Winking and walking to the proper locker room Sandy teases.

As she's gathering her things she realizes she has a missed call from her best friend Nina. She exits the building, parked in the first available spot next to handicap. Scrolling her contacts, she returns her best friend call the phone rings four times before Nina picks up.

Hello?

Wassup Bitch you called?

Had yo stankin ass answered the phone you wouldn't be asking me that what you doing hoe?

Chuckling. Girl chill I'm just leaving the gym.

Mhmm. I don't know why you always at that damn gym, it's not like its helping yo no curve having ass.

It's helping me just where I need it to.

And where exactly is that?

The men department.

Girl bye last time I checked you was baeless, soooo it's helping you how?

See that's where you wrong at I met bae today.

Girllll do he even know you exist?

Yesss! Bitch we made physical contact.

Bitch tell me you aint busting it open in the gym stalls.

Not yet at least he wouldn't let me.

The Fuck you mean? He wouldn't let you, so yo freak ass tried it? Do you even know him?

Didn't I just tell you that's bae?

In yo head or in real life? What's his name?

Tony.

Tony? Tony! As in T? Like Tiny man?

No, Tony as in T, as in my bae!

Girl, stop it! Now you're playing with fire.

He is fire! Sizzling hot just like I like them.

What's his role in all this? Y'all Fucking?

Who are you her private investigator? Or something. And nah, well not yet anyways.

Yet? Bitch don't catch another harassment case stalking that man. And you know Tiny is my client, so I've seen firsthand the damage she does to bitches about her man. Just let them be or this won't end well.

Ugh Bitch I gotta go you sure know how to fuck up my night with all this righteousness!

Ooh well girl bye! You know imma keep it G like it or not.

Both girls hang up their receivers.

The Layout

Tiny walks inside her hair salon, she had the place decked out and she designed it herself; plush chairs for awaiting customers along with free refreshments. Tiny truly appreciated her clients and she showed it often. From the comfort of her salon to the customer appreciation days and random gifts. Everything ranging from free salon services, to all-inclusive get-a-ways. She showed just as much appreciation to her employees.

There were four hairstylists, three nail techs, and two barbers working in Paradise. Tiny named it that because that's where you were inside her shop. On the right wall is Vee at the Secretary desk. Before making any arrangements or speaking to anyone you had to go through her. Vee was the glue to Paradise, she kept the place together, knowing everybody's business, always up on the latest gossip, staying on her toes and she aint take no shit. She never missed a beat, always at work and on time. Probably why it was so easy for her to keep up with the client names, appointments and pay schedules not to mention all the latest tea.

Next to the secretary desk sat an aquarium filled with tropical fish. In the right corner was a perfectly mounted 52-inch flat screen so waiting customers could have some entertainment from the front of the salon in their plush chairs.

Alongside the other wall, you have the four hairstylists in a row, against the back-left wall is where the three shampoo sinks sat. A walkway divided the two sides leading to the restrooms on the left side first was the women's restroom with two stalls, and two sinks. Next to it was the men's restroom having one stall, two urinals and two sinks. On the right was a storage room and next to it was Tiny back office.

In between the fish tank and TV were two steps leading to the two barbers, the twins Ronny and Rodney. It was damn near impossible to tell the two apart on the surface the gold tooth usually gave them away but it was hard to remember which side belonged to which twin. And that nasty cigarette and black and mild habit Rod had was a dead giveaway. Side by side they were the exact same person but on the inside, they were total opposites. One would question if they were even brothers, let alone twins. You could always catch them debating sports, politics, or which woman had the fattest ass. You could rarely hear them debating for the same side. Opposite side of them is where you got nailed by one of the three best nail techs in the city, Tisha, Kita, or Nina.

Tisha and Kita were both dope but they weren't fucking with Nina, she was on another level, from the shape, the strength and how she laid your polish. For those reasons, she was Tiny's personal tech she'd dabble time to time, but Nina was just her favorite. This silently caused tension between the three girls but it wasn't intentional.

Nina knew exactly how Tiny liked her nails and she kept her popping with the latest trends and colors.

Those stiletto nails were trendy. But Tiny wasn't a fan square her off. From time to time she'd let Nina convince her to rock the stilettos, and she never disappointed. Tita and Kita both felt as if she never gave them a long enough chance to prove themselves.

Although, Nina was her favorite she kept it on a professional level.

Tiny always offered advice when asked or she'd weigh in on controversial topics, but she never got personal. It wasn't unusual for the workers in the shop to link up and hang out but Tiny rarely engaged, apart from her dealings with Ron. Him and T been tight since high school so he was the only one welcomed in both aspects of her life. Tiny was a private person; if it was hers it was personal, it was sacred, therefore it had to be protected. She always knew how to separate business from personal and she had this mastered; therefore, personal issues didn't conflict with shop drama that was until she met Sandy.

Making Connections

Sandy grabs her water bottle and Ziploc bag packed with fruit, snatches her gym bag off the counter, and heads to the gym.

Sandy tosses her bag to the back turns up her music and pulls out. Merging on 75 South rapping aloud shouting the lyrics to the song all wrong. She exits and makes two lefts turns before arriving at the gym. Pulling in she instantly recognizes Tony truck and pulls into the available spot next to him. Gathering her belongings, she heads into the gym and straight into the lady's locker room. Sandy quickly dressed and put her gym bag inside her reserved locker number thirteen.

Hitting the gym floor, dressed in a hot pink and green sports bra with the matching compression shorts and running shoes, Sandy approaches a mirror analyzing herself as if it was her first time seeing her reflection. Quickly stretching she grabs two 10lb dumbbells and proceed to squat. After completing 100 squats she gets on the treadmill.

This was Sandy's daily routine; she came up with her own workout plan in hopes for a curvy body.

The treadmill is set for 45 minutes, Sighing, *I need some motivation*, as she plugs her headphones into her mp3 player and turns the music up. Fifteen minutes into her run Sandy looks around as if she's searching for a lost child.

She suddenly hears this deep voice. "It works every time."

An annoyed Sandy responds, your point? What you mean by that?

I mean you've been breaking your neck to see where I was and I've been next to you this entire time your focus was watching out for me and not yourself and your surroundings that's how people end up hurt.

Well lots of people watch me! I mean look at me. As she's rubbing her hands up and down her body.

Shaking his head back and forth, he replies. You're as dumb as I thought. You think it's OK for someone to be that close to you without you knowing? T, chuckling and shaking his head back and forth at her.

Cute, but I think that's minimal when you've known their every move well before they even knew you existed.

Yo, you are crazy like for real. Something is really wrong with you. Didn't yo parents teach you no means no?

Nah! My parents taught me to go for what I want and that sometimes people don't know what they want until you give it to them.

It's apparent you've been fucked up since birth, enjoy being crazy I'm, out.

She sucks her teeth. Mhmm see you Tuesday, same time.

Around noon, Tiny walks to her back office and take a few deep breaths. After all the latest commotion with the police war on black people, it began affecting Tiny physically especially hearing all the different opinions fly around the shop. Her head was throbbing due to an onset of a migraine. She grabs a few things and heads to the front.

Tiny needed a break from the shop she was tired of hearing all the latest political debating, and watching her brothers and sister getting gunned down by the police everyday became too much for her to handle. Not to mention all of the carrying on in the shop. She decided to take an extended lunch and head home for a while.

Yo, Vee! I'm headed out the shop for a couple hours please make sure everything stay together and these fools don't kill one another while I'm out.

Tiny you know I got you, but if you want me to close we'll be shutting down early you know I gotta get out of here by 6:30.

I'll be back by then, I just need some food, and fresh air.

Alright now, Bye! Get out of here. Paradise is in great hands.

I know you know you run this place probably better than me. Tiny exits the shop and heads home not before stopping at the Coney Island a few miles from home she couldn't go in without getting her fix; wing dinner with chili and cheese on the fries.

They knew her by first name and knew exactly what she was ordering because she ordered the same thing every time she went. She pulled into her driveway and realized Tony was home as well. Thus, she decided to sit in the car and finish off her food.

Surprises are Always Fun

Shaking his head rushing to his car, T hits his unlock button twice, jump in the driver seat, turned up his radio and rushed home. The gym was about twenty minutes away from home. He wanted to get home and prepare his surprise for his lady, T set up an in-home massage for her, when she was leaving the shop, Ronny was instructed to call T so he'd be on point with everything. T pulls into his driveway, exits the car and follows his pathway to the end of the street where his mailbox sat. T opens the mailbox grabs the contents inside out and proceeds up his walkway into the house.

He slides his keys on the landing as well as his mail. Runs up the stairs to his closet; opens his drawers, grabs a t-shirt and a pair of boxers. Tony walks into the shower, fifteen minutes later T turns the nozzle till the water shuts off. Pulling back the shower curtain he extends his arms and grabs his towel from the rack, wraps it around his waist, roll it and tuck it as he steps onto their all white plush rug. Water rolling down every inch of his body making all his muscles glow, especially his calf's they were cut so deep and were perfectly proportioned. He grabs his boxers and steps into them, and then slings his shirt over his shoulders as he picks up and puts up his dirty clothes.

T walks in the room, grabs the remote, kick his leg on the bed while his other leg slightly hangs off.

He turns on ESPN Chicago vs. Indiana. *Let's go Rose lets go Butler dub these niggas!* T was a die-hard Chicago fan being that was his home town; no matter how bad they sucked he'd still tune in, root for his team and swear they were gone win the championship every year.

Come on now we gone start off strong and finish strong we need tight D.. T shouts at the TV as if he's the assistant coach and they can hear him. To his surprise in walks Tiny.

Wassup baby you alright? Cuz you look like you seen a ghost.

It's just that I wasn't expecting you till later

So, who the fuck was you expecting then?

Not this shit again crazy I wasn't expecting nobody and specially not yo ass you posed to be at the shop baby.

Mhmm, whatever nigga. I slipped off early they were getting on my nerves so I decided to take a long lunch and see what you were up to.

Waiting on my side chick and watching Wade bust Indiana ass.

She snatches his towel off and throw it at him. "Stupid!" I heard yo loud ass outside the door. As she takes a seat next to him, Tony tries to fill Tiny out to see if she's hip at all because he hadn't heard from Ronny. I only got like an hour and a half before the place goes up in flames.

You miss me, don't you? As T pulls her on top of him and grips her ass. You worry too much sometimes just relax as he kisses her deeply massaging his tongue with hers as if they were still in high school.

Tiny chuckles, you miss me I see as she looks down at an erect T.

He looks off shyly. Nope, no, I don't.

Well somebody told me otherwise!

Really, who?

Him, as Tiny slides her hand down her man chest hitting every inch of his muscle until she's off him and on her knees.

He grabs the back of her head and stares deeply into her eyes. I fucking love you.

She looks up into his eyes as to say, I already know, before taking every inch of him in her mouth.

Damn girl. You better chill, T moans. She spits a glob of slob, still tickling his head with the back of her throat. Up and down in and out spit, suck, swallow, in a routine manner. He massages her hair while pushing her head further and further down, as he's literally fucking her throat seconds before exploding in the back of it. Rising to her feet Tiny softly utters, I love you too, without an inch of evidence present.

Walking to the bathroom she is quickly interrupted by a grasp of the wrist and before she could respond she was tossed on the bed, I KNOW You aint think you was getting off that easy? As he's sliding down her panties from under her skirt. But I, I gotta get back, I gotta make sure they don't kill each other and everybody was busy tonight, so I gotta close the shop.

Mhmm. As he places his finger over her lips.

I know, as Tony Lay beside her. He begins kissing her neck and licking inside her earlobe whispering get on top. Tiny gazing, caught up in the moment until T shifts her focus, you heard me, Get yo ass up here.

Finally following orders, she climbs on top of his chest. He begins guiding her with his forearms until his arms locked inside her inner thighs. He goes to work licking every inch of his lady.

Flicking his tongue back and forth sliding in and out of her wetness, she starts thrusting her hips against him, rocking back and forth but that only excited him more.

She began heavy panting, her legs shaking as she's trying to get off he pulls her right back onto his face, this time with a tighter grip, she's moaning, shaking uncontrollably and screaming. I'm bouta cum I'm bouta to cum, as she shoots right in Tony nose. He slows down but doesn't stop nor does he let her move. Trying to muster up the words nothing but moans will come out while she collapsed on his chest.

He chuckles. You know what it feels like to have your soul removed now.

She playfully hits him that was involuntary manslaughter.

He rubs his fingers through her hair, only thing I slaughtered is that pussy, as he throws her off him.

You aint do shit! Tiny says jokingly while twirling her hair through her two fingers and softly kicking her legs back and forth. So, you still aint learned huh? I know what to do for you.

As T gets up and kneels over his woman admiring every inch of her smooth chocolate skin before kissing her perfectly in the center of back. He instantly sent chills through Tiny's body making her nipples stand firm and at attention.

Bae nooo, stop I really gotta get back.

No, you don't. You good. I hit Ronny and told him what to do he said him and Rod got you.

You did what? Tony, you know how I am.

Yeah, I do but you heard me. Now hush; let me handle this. The shop is fine. He rolls over on top and lays a wet one on tiny before lowering and tongue kissing her juice box.

Just seconds before he slid every one of his 10 inches inside of her; what's that shit you was talking earlier? He asks as he's going deeper and deeper.

Tiny begins re-positioning herself, stretches her arms until they are gripping the end of the bed, and rise her ass further up until it's straight up in the air. Looking back at her man as to say, Nigga you heard me.

Licking her lips and winking, amps him up even more he smacks her ass as he's pounding her like he is in a royal rumble. Huh? Ion hear you! T shouts as Tiny Moans louder and louder.

Tiny realizing Tony is winning this round, she began thrusting her hips rocking back and forth making that ass bounce up and down. Ooohh, ahhh, ummm... deeper baby go deeper.

She began taking control reaching under her legs and tickling his balls, this sent T over the top.

Pulling out dick still rock solid and dripping. Gripping her left leg tosses on her stomach grabbing her with a fist full of hair as he inserts tiny stretches, he shifts insides. Ooh Tony, Tony Waiiiitt he's getting the best of her as she begins slipping off the side of the bed. This doesn't slow him down one bit. Wanting so bad to regain control Tiny slides off the bed and is in a full-blown head stand. She begins fiercely working her muscles then whispers, This pussy yours.

It's whose?

All yours, as the both explode in ecstasy together they collapse and drift off.

The Link Up: PART ONE TINY!

Nov 14, 2008

Tiny drifts off reminiscing about the first time she met Tony. It was a rainy day on campus. Tiny wakes up, shower, and made a smoothie before heading out for her morning jog to campus. She decided to spend the day unwinding after finishing her final midterm. Stretching before, taking off dressed in a yellow zip up hoodie, and black yoga pants with the matching shoes.

Reaching campus, Tiny stops and does a quick shake off, you know the little routine you do after a good run; (bounce up and down, crossing your arms back and forth, moving your neck side to side, just before saying whew) heading into the café. After making her way to the grill line, she orders her a cheeseburger and fries.

How are you having that? the cook asked.

 Well done with everything on it cut in half and season the fries a familiar voice called out.

I see you still remember Antonius, Tiny states with her back still turned.

He grabs her shoulder so she'd turn and face him. How could I forget? He asks.

Well, probably because we haven't spoken since freshmen year. Dang it's been dat long asking Tonius?

Rolling her eyes while punching him in the arm. Yea it's been dat long.

Ouuchh! what was that for baby girl?

One, I aint yo baby girl. Two, cuz how the fuck three whole years pass and you don't even know we aint spoke? You aint check on me or nothing?

Can't check on a ghost. T states sarcastically. What are you even doing here anyways I thought you were at Northwestern?

Ma'am your order is up. She lifts her tray and turns to the drinking fountain. He grabs her tray as she fills her cup up with Sweet tea. As the two scan the café looking for an open table; spotting one on the far-left side of the cafeteria the two make their way to the table. They were even lucky enough to snag a booth. So, what's new with you Antonius?

Tony starts laughing. Stop calling out my government girl.

Ok Tonius! Tiny snaps back. what's new?

Nothing Tinyesha!

Ooh no you didn't go there Artavius.

Stop playing with me girl. Tony tosses a fry at her. Nah for real tho same ol same ole you know hitting these books and hooping what about you? You still dancing and cheering?

Yea, I'm still dancing. I got tryouts today at six.

Tryouts? You always were a distraction.

The two shared laughs.

Nah rather I was on the sideline or in the game I was rooting for you to win!

Yea Yea whatever I'll catch up with you later tho I gotta head over to the gym.

Alright, later Antonius

Later Tiny.

Tiny heads over to tryouts immediately following the coach pulled her to the side and offered her a partial scholarship leaving the gym ecstatic she bumps into Tony leaving out the gym door!

Congrats baby girl! He said I'm glad you can keep rooting me on!

I can't cheer for you if you riding the bench!

The two shared a few laughs then began to part ways.

Lemme get home tho call me later?

Now you know better! You need A ride?

NO Tony. I'm fine!

Promise to take you straight home! T says teasingly with the corner of his lips twisted and turned up!

Tinyesha admired his devilish grin that was one of the many things she admired about him. No, I ran here. I need to run back so I can stay in shape.

Girl you are fine ok. Let's make a bet we race to that light pole if I beat you we ride—

And when you lose?

If I lose we run either way you're not going alone.

He pushes her and takes off Tinyesha takes off yelling, "nope you cheated it doesn't count!" Reaching the light pole seconds after him "nope it doesn't count you cheated and I still almost beat you!"

This aint horseshoes woman.

Well let's race to the car!

For what now?

Just to prove I'm faster than you.

Maybe another day take your loss like a champ.

Pulling into the women's dorm parking lot, Tony pulls up to the curb and put the car in park as the two begin reminiscing back on their younger days and when they first met.

Do you remember that day at the park where you were playing? Me and Sherri were dancing and just because that boy said "Damn girl," you threw the ball at him! Had the whole court fighting over nothing!

Tony lets off a slight laugh. That wasn't for nothing. I fight for what's mine always remember that and just like you were mine then, you're mine now.

Tinyesha turns her head. Hmmh. I aint agree to that.

You didn't have to. He leans in and began kissing her.

Tony phone began vibrating for the hundredth time fucking up the mood, sending a steaming Tiny to her boiling point she pushes him away from her and snatches his phone:

"Can't wait to see you tonight" with heart eyes appeared in a message. Jealousy and rage brewing inside a pissed off Tiny responds.

"SORRY PLANS CHANGED AND FROM THIS DAY FORTH DON'T TEXT THIS PHONE I GOT A GIRL AND IM JUST TRYING TO BE HAPPY WITH HER."

She tosses the phone at him. Who the fuck is this and why in the entire fuck do she think she seeing you tonight? Ooh I Swear to fucking God Tony!!

He laughs. You're still crazy. That's my roommate's sister and I gotta pick him up from her house why you over there mad for no reason, always jumping to conclusions crazy ass!

Well IS HE DEAF OR FUCKING BLIND OR DO I LOOK LIKE IM DUMB?

WAIT. WHAT where that come from?

IM JUST TRYNA FIGURE OUT WHAT THE FUCK SO IMPORTANT AT TEN O'clock at night AND WHY THE FUCK SHE TEXTING YOU HIS HANDS BROKE?

Look chill we got business to handle and that's where he told me to get him from! And I gave her my number a while ago.

He must've told her I was coming tonight so she texted me. We talked a time or two and no I never fucked her happy?

Oh well! You should've. You better tell him you NOT coming; he better walk.

You're real demanding! Two years ago, right?

She rolls her eyes. Whatever, bye. Go see yo lil bitch den. As Tiny reaches for the handle he pulls her back in as the car instantly grew silent.

What's wrong?

Reaching to unfold Tiny arms,

NOTHING!!

Yeah ok, if I recall correctly you broke up with me.

Well! A lot was going on obviously more than you could deal with.

Look I don't want to dwell on the past but did you fuck that nigga at yo room that day?

Tiny burst into tears. Fuck you! There never was a nigga at no room with me are you fucking serious you still never let this go?

Well why were you so paranoid and who the fuck did you get the pistol from?

My fucking daddy; the night I lost them I went to clear my head so I got a room. Matter of fact how the fuck you know that?

The nigga you pulled a pistol was my little homie JJ, he texted me and told me you were there but by the time I got there you were gone.

That's because his dumb ass scared me I didn't know what to do I just loss everything and then I loss you too.

Noticing Tiny tears still rolling down her face, Tony leans over and begins wiping them. Finally unfolding her arms, he gets her full attention. Look at me. Still looking away he grabs her face, LOOK AT ME! Staring in each other's eyes. THANKS.

Thanks? With a look of confusion, Thanks for?

Taking me back!

Boy who told you that?

YOU and I love how you let me know!

Looking at him out the corner of her eyes whatever! Like I said, Go and see your little girlfriend ok?

Tony exits the car.

What are you doing?

I'm going to see my girl she stay in these dorms.

Oh, ok tell her you still in love with me!

Dumb ass.

Yeah alright.

Entering the building together they split ways at the stairs Tiny reaches her room to find it empty as it was most nights her roommate stayed out. She sat on the edge of her bed and replayed the day events instantly getting mad remembering her and her man just entered her dorm building together but why the fuck wasn't he at her room? Tiny thoughts began racing. *Who the fuck does he know? What bitch he fucking? Probably every little bitch here I swear I'm killing him, her, and Imma set this whole dorm on fire watch me!*

Tiny shouts as if someone is in the room with her. *I know bitches throwing it at him.* She jumps to her feet and began pacing back and forth growing more and more heated by the second. After 5 maybe 10 minutes of ranting a knock at the door quiets her down. Her insides tingling as she tries hard to fight back her excitement expecting it to be her boo. Confirming it was him threw the peephole she slings the door open.

Who the fuck is she? and where the fuck she at so I can go let her know wassup.

Ooh you gone let her know huh? T says with a half smirk and a look in his eyes that said I want you as he pulls something from behind his back.

Birds chirping. All you could hear was- Tweet, Tweet, Tweet, Tweet. Tiny is awakened by her alarm. While T didn't budge She double checks the time. It was six p.m. *Ooh shit I gotta get back to the shop.*

She takes a quick shower and texts Vee to let her know she was on her way before heading out to the shop.

RUFFLE SOME FEATHERS

Putting her plan in motion, she jumps in her all black 300 and began mapping out this twisted plan to claim what she felt like was hers. Looking down at her hand, *I sure could use a Mani might as well go for both.* Pulling up to her destination she is greeted by this Short brown-skin dude with a scruffy face and a gold tooth but it was something about his accent that intrigued Sandy.

Hello Miss, in this deep Chicago accent.

Hey! As she bypasses him.

He admires her and watches her every move through the glass doors.

Sandy walks inside of paradise around their busiest time 6:30 and request the best nail tech in here.

I've been hearing about her.

Vee instantly get this uneasy feeling she began pretending to look over the paperwork. Do you have an appointment?

I didn't think I needed one, Sandy snaps

Well you do and all our nail techs are booked for the day would you like to set an appointment?

No I would like to speak with A nail tech please.

Um, they are all with a client and they are all booked but you can come back and get the same response or you can set your appointment.

You know what lemme get out of here before I smack me A bitch.

Vee steps around the desk and gets in her face. What bitch you talking about?

As the two gets closer and closer the argument is getting more intense and seemingly is about to turn physical. Everybody immediately stopped what they were doing to tune into the drama as the workers come between the two.

Tiny comes from the back. Excuse me. What's going on up here?

Ask yo rude ass assistant, Sandy snaps at Tiny.

BIHHH Vee said snatching herself. Girl I'll show you rude.

Come on Vee Akita grabs Vee and take her to the back.

This bitch don't know. Kita, I will stomp her ass.

Who is she anyway.

Bitch aint spent a dime in here and come in like she the fucking owner. The owner don't even do all that.

Iono but I don't trust that bitch. It's something fishy about her.

Tiny knowing Vee only gets out of character when it's called for. She gives her a look of reassurance letting her know that You good. I'll handle it from here.

Kita, you got an opening? Not even acknowledging Tiny's question. Tiny moves on.

Nina, is it possible for you to squeeze a client in? Nina steaming hot, but manages to keep it under control she sarcastically asks, what are you trying to get done ma'am?

An overlay and a Pedi.

Sorry, I can't today but you can come first thing in the morning!

What time? I have A few appointments tomorrow

8 a.m. is my only available time, knowing Sandy didn't like mornings

OK that's fine. Make sure y'all put y'all pit bull on a leash in the morning.

Tiny intervenes. Just like I ask my employees to respect customers, my customers must respect my employees or find services elsewhere. This is a drama free zone.

Oh, OK what's your name?

Tiny dismissing her question, forcing Nina to respond.

Nina. Yours?

Cassandra!

OK Cassandra. See you in the morning 8am.

She exits and before she was out the door. She had a paragraph for a text message.

Bitch the fuck are you doing making a scene this my motherfucking job how I eat keep that shit in the streets whatever sick ass game you playing don't interfere with how me and my kids eat. Yo god kids grow the fuck up shit aint cute at fuckin all. Bitch you bet not come up here no more or I ain't fuckin with you I'm comfortable here and you not about to fuck this up cuz of a dick obsession.

Rod still outside smoking and admiring her he decided to shoot his shot. Can I call you later miss lady?

Um I don't know, can you?

Well if you give me your number I'm sure I would.

He walks over to her and opens her car door. So, is that a yes miss lady?

Give me yours and I'll call you!

Don't play with me ill come find you if you don't.

That statement got Sandy on the hook.

I'm Sand and you?

Rod!

Ok Mr. Rod What time will you be leaving the shop?

Round bout 8 why?

I'll be ready by 9 ill text my address later.

This brought Rod to a smile showing his open face gold tooth. I like yo style lil mama. I'll get up with you later if you aint bullshitting. He closed her door.

Shouting from her window, don't be late, as she sped off.

Vee watched the whole scene from her desk in disgust. *Something aint right with this girl* she thought *and Imma find out exactly what it is.*

Sandy laughing to herself, knowing this is all a part of her twisted plan, she texts Nina back.

Girl chill it's so much more than a dick obsession but you right. I'm sorry I won't come to your job again or piss off your boss. Well, at least not in Paradise. Love you bf ttyl.

Rod finally returning after his prolonged smoke break he takes his next client come on J. The chatter fills the shop everybody from clients, workers, to patrons just hanging out were discussing the incident that just unfolded. Everything from the, "who was she", "what happened." to "I wanted Vee to knock her ass out" could be heard across the shop.

Lil J, who was one of Rod's regulars, said: That's Sandy from around the way. She always into it with somebody and always fucking a different nigga. Any nigga with money she after or already had. I used to smash back in the day but the hoe was always cheating.

Rod asked, you sure you aint just mad cuz she don't give you play no more?

Man Naw. That bitch the devil. Money is all she cares about.

Rod taking everything in.

Ooh, exactly what I thought! A rat bitch! Vee shouted. But I'm pulling the Nikes out tomorrow. We will see if the bitch bout it in the morning.

Oh unun. Paid half day off for you ma'am. Ion need you to catch another case, especially for a classless, worthless, hood rat.

But Tee.

Nope. Be here by 12 tomorrow. Not a minute before.

Nina shaking her head knowing everything that was being said was true. She decides to chime in, I hope she cancel her appointment. That aint gone help her. She better hope Ion catch her rat ass on the street.

Lil J said: That's the easiest place to catch her. She always hanging out on 7mile, and the car wash.

7 mile? Rod asked.

Yeah. You know, over there by the freeway where that car wash at.

Vee nodding her head thanks J, it's noted. Rod don't you stay over there somewhere?

Nah, I stay on 8mile and in the opposite direction.

THE REMATCH: PART 2 TONY!

Tony smiling in his sleep with that same feeling he had on that rainy day when she became his woman. Was this another sign? Interrupted by a ring on his phone, Tony stretches his arms from under his pillow, and feels for his phone.

Incoming call from Ronny. YO bro what's the word?

It's a go I'm getting ready to shut everything down here and have everybody at the spot by 8, right?

Yea.

But hold up. Bae! Tony yells out. Bae? He gets up and realizes their home is only occupied by him.

You know what that mean?

Yea, her ass don't listen.

They both laugh she'll be there soon. I'm sure she don't think y'all can operate on y'all own I see. Don't shut down. Let her, but everything else proceeds as normal. You help her close and make sure she gets there. I'll have her clothes with me.

Aight.

For sho!

One!

One!

He ends the call shaking his head. Smiling *her ass don't listen.* Slipping out of bed he heads to take a quick shower, removing his clothes from the closet he begins getting dressed he puts on some gray slacks, a light blue shirt, with a black and blue bow tie paired with shoes to match. He reaches down and pulls out a big box hidden at the bottom of the closet. He set it on the bed with the note still attached "Meet me at Joes grill on 7th at 9pm."

He dialed Ron. Wassup bro! She there?

Yea. Cussing everybody out as usual.

Alright look I'm bouta slide up there and put the shit in her car. Keep her away from the front.

He takes one last look in the mirror and pulls this small box out of his pocket. He opens it and began admiring it. Thinking back to the day he knew he wanted her by his side forever and this time was no different.

Standing outside her dorm after a quick trip to the campus store to get some of her favorite snacks. He just left her to believe he was sliding to another chick room. All the while he was admiring every inch of her frown and holding on to all her vulgar words only thinking and dreaming of the day he can finally marry the girl who has been in his corner.

Thoughts piercing his mind. *No matter what path I was on, my shorty was there meeting me half way. Rather I deserved it or not, I never felt so connected with another person, and this had to be fate, here she was again unexpectedly sitting in my car spazzing on me about a girl I aint even gave a second thought to. I haven't even heard from her since her parents' funeral.*

And although we hadn't been together for quite some time, that never stopped us for feeling as if we belonged to each other. Maybe we are really destined to be. This gotta be what true love was but how can I make this right?

Would this be all for you sir?

And some of those too.

Your total comes up 10.60 the cashier says.

Tony pays for his bag of snacks and heads back up to her room. With this beautiful figure standing in front of him going off, he got turned on by the second. All that was going through his mind was, *I know I want her in my life forever and tonight that pussy was mine.*

Tiny cursing him out. Still he walked in and closed the door with one hand behind his back. Now, kick yo own ass. You're the girl I'm coming to see goofy ass girl, as he hands Tiny, her snack bag.

She empties it on her desk. Aww baby. Thank you. You remembered Strawberry Fanta, Hot Cheeto Puffs, Hot fries, Sour Patches, and Starbursts. Like a big kid, she jumps in his arms and began kissing him. Tony puts her on the bed.

What time is your roommate coming back?

She isn't till tomorrow.

He began kissing her softly on her neck and follows to her nipple. He sucks her breast back and forth for a few moments before heading down to her stomach. Tiny asked nervously. What are you doing?

Something I should've done A long time ago shhhhhh. He began kissing her inner thighs and bites at her panties. Squirming, helping him slide them down, he places his face to her box licking all around. Tony began sucking on her clitoris and working two fingers in and out her pussy. She began creaming over his fingers shaking uncontrollably. Antonius rolls on his back, come here and put it on my face, enjoy the ride. She does just that, climbed on top and rocked back and forth controlling her pace until she reached her climax.

Tony locks her legs and takes over causing Tiny to go into what she describes as a shock; shaking uncontrollably, unable to speak and a complete loss of control. She squirts up his nose.

Damn girl you tryna drown a nigga. He climbs on top of her and begin kissing her in her mouth. I love you Tinyesha.

I love you too. She grabs his waist and tugs at his zipper.

T stops and sat on the edge of the bed. Are you sure about this? I don't want to rush you and you know I don't mind waiting for you.

I want you, is all Tiny could manage to say.

Tony strips butt naked and climbs on top of her as he pokes at her hole.

Wait a minute do you have protection?

He goes to his pocket began giving her head again and putting on the condom at the same time he pokes at Tiny again. This time a little further, does it hurt he ask?

A little.

He slides in her again.

Ouch.

Do you want me to stop?

Nooo. Don't stop. He goes in again. Tiny, more comfortable this time.

Does it hurt still? Tiny ignores him. Tony keeping this slow stroke up for about 8 minutes before he came. Tiny began feeling as if he now belonged to her and she belonged to him, not only now but forever.

So, did you enjoy it? Tonius asks

Still shaking, she lets out a giggle what you think? I might've.

Smacking his lips, yeah aight. You good over there I see you still shaking.

She pushes him. Whatever.

The two stayed up reminiscing about their past and planning their futures. The conservation bounced from the times she's caught him cheating, to the girls she beat up, the time she got locked up for stomping one of his sidelines out in front of the whole school, to the time he grabbed her up in front of the whole school because she was play fighting in the hallway with another nigga. And him setting her secret admirer on fire in the bathroom. Sharing all their crazy moments had the two of them feeling as if they were destined to be. They concluded that no matter what they'd always be friends and have each other back but they still hadn't resolved the issue of who was crazier. Before they knew it, it was 5am T began gathering his things.

Just where the fuck are you going?

To my room. I got practice today.

Nice try. You got practice tonight. You know how I know? Because we got the gym before y'all.

Taking a deep breath with a look of confusion on his face.

Um what is it? What's wrong, talk to me as she grabs his hands.

Nothing it's just that I wanted to get comfortable without making you uncomfortable.

Um ok?

I sleep naked and I don't want you to feel like I'm rushing you or pressuring you into anything.

Laughing, boy I den woke up with dick on my back before. Lay down you'll be okay.

The room went completely silent, so quiet you can hear your thoughts out loud. What seemed like hours was only seconds before a pissed off Tony lashed out. The fuck you mean? Who the fuck you sleeping naked with?

She burst out in rapid laughter mimicking him. The fuck you mean?

Man, stop fucking playing with me I don't see shit funny for real.

Boy chill the fuck out it's a joke. Tiny shouts still laughing

Yea alright I'm out!

Byeee! Tell yo lil bitch I said hello.

Yup. I will Tony walks out and slam the door. Tiny quickly following behind him, she grabs his wrist to turn him to face her. Damn it's that easy?

Frowned up. Naw but are you?

Am I what? As she folds her arms, you know what? Never mind don't answer that.

Tiny feeling ultimately disrespected after just giving herself to her man. She began shouting I find it real fucking funny you can fuck bitches left and right but can't take a joke.

Yo chill the fuck out.

No fuck that you on some bullshit probably doing all of this to go lay up with another bitch any way.

Tony push Tiny back in the room and pulls her in closer to him. Come here, baby I'm sorry. I was wrong, but you already know how I get! I'll kill any nigga who even think of touching you. So, don't fucking play with me.

But you can fuck who you want though?

Look stop saying that I know I fucked up in the past. I was younger then. Things are different now. I know who I want and I finally got her.

Don't make me fuck you up Antonius, as she kisses him.

I'm not, he whispers. I love you too much.

Grabbing his keys and her gifts he exits his house. **Five minutes out,** he texts Ronny to let him know he's close.

Ron respond **ok it's a go!**

You sure?

Yeah, she in the back, counting the money. Everybody else knows what time and where to be Imma gone head and head up there.

What you mean bro? You gotta keep an eye on her.

Nigga, Rod got it!

I gotta go handle the business and meet the DJ at the grill.

Rod? I hope he don't fuck this up. You know he antsy and Tiny don't like him but alright, bet. I'll see you there.

Tony parks down the street and walks up to Tiny's car using the spare key on his key ring. He places her gift in the passenger seat and quietly close her door. Making his way back to his car, he texts to let Ron know it's all good and he was headed to the spot.

Tiny's Surprise

Tony pulls up to Joes Grill. It was one of Tiny's favorite spots and they had the best sushi in town. Ronny was instructed to rent the building out for the entire night so it'll be a private party. Everybody from the shop was in attendance, along with their mates. Both of Tony's brothers Anthony and Antwan came through and Tiny's sisters/closest friends.

Sherri, Tiny's other half, flew in the night before and helped with decorating of her dinner. Tony walks in where he is first greeted by Ron. The two slap fives and pat each other on the back. In the same motion, the two exchanged envelopes.

Tony whispers to Ron, Thanks bro for everything.

Wassup brother from another! Sherri shouts while walking towards him.

Hey sis. Thanks for coming down and helping me keep this secret.

She doesn't suspect a thing.

You sure? Cuz you know she hard to surprise.

Yeah. I know but I took care of that.

When is the last time you talked to her?

Two days ago, before I left. Don't worry I aint ruin the surprise.

Just checking you know how y'all do.

Lol whatever.

"Fuck jokes aint shit funny when talk shit about make sure you say Im getting money."-Nisha Blanco plays over Ri's phone speaker. This her right here, shh as she makes her way outside.

Hello? Wassup sis!

Hey. What's going on?

Nothing what you up to?

Nothing much girl waiting on dinner to finish so I can eat.

Oh, what you cook?

Some steak, shrimp, and potatoes ooh I can't forget about my cheddar bay biscuits.

Damn I need to be there.

Yeah. You overdue for a visit and you missing my birthday.

I know Imma come visit soon. But girl I called to tell you about this hood rat that came popping off in the shop today.

Wait what happened?

Ahhh!!! Tiny screams in the phone as she realizes the box, rose, and the note attached to it.

Bitch what the fuck? Are you ok?

Hold on?

No girl. What's going on? Sounding concerned

Girl yes. Let me call you back I gotta run in here and get dressed.

Unun. Bitch and go where?

Girl I don't know Tony bought me something and left a note with an address.

Ooh shit girl you think tonight is the night?

Ooh shit I don't know, but I will never find out if Iono get dressed. I'll call you when I'm back in the car.

OK talk to you later. Bye Bye.

The call ends as Tiny walks through her front door.

Tiny jumps up as she reads the note:

> *To My Queen, I know you've been working hard lately. It's time to relax and let me show you how much I appreciate you. Put this on and meet me at your favorite restaurant by 9:30. I made reservations for us.*
>
> *Signed,*
>
> *Your King*

She opens the box where she finds a custom dress from her favorite company TPF imprints. With some black and blue leather boots to match, this black and blue custom bodycon dress.

Inside of the shoe box, she notices a smaller box that had a 2.5 karat, white gold choker with the matching earrings and a bracelet.

T went all out to show his appreciation for his boo.

She removes her new pieces, holds them in place, checking them out in the mirror. Making sure everything matched. She laid everything across the bed before heading to the shower. Tiny steps into the shower letting the steaming hot water run down her back, she drifts off into a fantasy as she starts visualizing and anticipating the night ahead. She knew Tony had been acting strange but had assumed the worse. The surprise caught her off guard.

She gets out the shower and instantly texts Ri.

What if this the night he proposed?

Um Iono Tee you think he is. If he does, are you ready?

Idk this just really caught me off guard. Its random as fuck and I don't know I'm prolly overreacting,

Yeah don't put too much thought into it, just enjoy your night. Love you. Text me when you make it.

K! I'm bouta get dressed. I'll be calling you tomorrow with the deets.

First, the earrings; then she slips into her dress. It complimented every inch of her small thick frame. Sitting on the bed right foot first, she slides her boots on then zips them all the way up. She stands up for a final look before she applies her new neck piece and rolls on her lip gloss. She blows a kiss in the mirror. *Mwah!*

Admiring herself and the fact that her boo did good with her entire outfit.

Tiny heads to the closet and pulls out her blue and black leather jacket that matched perfectly with her boots and her bag. She made sure she had everything. She took one last look and heads out.

Tiny put the address in her GPS to be 100 percent sure she wouldn't make a wrong turn. Twenty minutes before arrival is what the GPS showed. Tiny cut her radio up and began cruising. She made a right turn into the restaurant. After parking, Tiny looks around and notices the only car there besides hers was Tony's.

He walks up to her door with a dozen of roses. As he opens it and assists his lady out, he hands the roses to her and admires her.

Damn girl, he said just before kissing her and grabbing a handful of ass. I love yo ass for real.

Tiny responds I love you too! in the softest voice imaginable. What you up to? Tiny asks. It bet not be nothing crazy.

Well I can't promise it aint nothing crazy but I got you.

Whatever!

As the two lock hands and began walking up to the restaurant, Tony pulls the door open as Tiny steps inside. T came in after and led the way. Moving from the front entrance to the back room where they hosted big parties of people.

I hope you brought your appetite. I know how much you love this, so I hope you enjoy it. Tony pushes through the double doors with Tiny close behind. Soo babe what do you think? Do you like it?

Tiny looking around as she spots the sushi bar loaded with a variety of sushi. The grill, where the chef was preparing whatever meat ordered and a full bar; in addition to a dessert table. What's the occasion? she asks with a raised eyebrow.

Love! Duh what you think?

I love it babe! Thanks, you're the best, as she turns and kisses him.

Tiny heard a familiar voice but doesn't turn around. She was still caught up in the moment with her man.

Tiny! with a tap on her shoulders. This time, the voice much closer, Um excuse ma'am!

Ahh bitch you posed to be home cooking and shit. Lying heffa.

Omg sis! It's been forever, but you know I gotta pay you back for this. Y'all got me good. Imma get his ass too.

As the three walked to their actual dining area, they were greeted by more family and friends. Tiny stunned. Wait! Now I know why all y'all was acting funny. I aint suspect this though.

The waiters came over with different trays of sushi and mixed drinks. They served the couple first. Tiny wanting to get away quickly; Where's the restroom?

Down the hall to the left the waiter responds.

Tiny turned to Sherri. Sherri walk with me.

As the two stands and exits.

Girl so how has life been? Ri asks.

Chile skip that. I'm nervous.

About what?

I think he's finally gonna propose.

And if he does? You ready?

Yeah, I mean I guess so.

What you mean you guess so?

Well you know we don't have a clean past and sometimes they revisit.

Girl bye! Show me a couple who do and that aint stopped you from loving him this long. What's the real tea?

I still don't trust him. I feel like he up to no good now and well--.

Damn really? Are you being insecure or what? Wait bitch who back?

Tiny responds you know what, never mind! Let's go enjoy this night.

Ri stops her from leaving, look sis I know you scared, but I also know that T loves you and he wanted to show you. Look around, he went out his way.

I swear to God if it's something you not telling me we beefing.

Girl yo nosey ass! It's already hard to surprise you and he pulled it off. So, let's go take some shots, eat some sushi, and live in the moment. Tomorrow we can have our girl's day and you can rant and bitch all you need to.

You promise?

Yes. I promise. You know I always got yo back. Now let's get back to the party.

Knowing Sherri meant what she said it was no question, that she would always have her back.

Who's Getting Surprised?

I was starting to think y'all got lost. Tony states jokingly. But then, I remembered its thing one and thing two together and they don't know how to shut up.

Whatever! Tiny asks. Where's yo shadow?

My shadow?

Yeah, the one you can't function without.

Ron?

Yeah.

Ron prolly handling some last-minute business. He helped me pull all of this off.

Tiny gets a text from Ron. **Walk outside and get in the black truck parked in front**. She gets up and walks from the table passing by Ri, she updates her. She states to her she'd be right back and that she was going out front for a minute. Tiny jumps inside the car and the driver handed her a small red box.

Sis I got something to ask before tonight over. Ron said from the front seat.

 I just gotta know after all these years did you know it wasn't me?

I knew when I dried my eyes that it wasn't you. I told Tony about it I'm surprised yall never talked about it. Did you want it to be?

Man hell naw, I don't look at you like that, but I always wondered did you know.

Duh you're my little big brother how would I not know? That's why I can't stand his ass till this day.

Ok cool I just had to be sure sis.

Did you think I would?

Nah! I knew better I just had to be sure. Because I know my brother.

Let me get back in this party bro. We missing all the fun.

Aight!

Come here sis! Let me show you something, T calls to Ri as he retrieves the yellow envelope from his inside jacket pocket. He also pulled out a small red box from the pocket too.

Sherri screams and tears roll down her face. Omg I'm so happy for her!!! I knew it! Talking about you, just wanted to throw her an appreciation dinner.

Yea. Well you know y'all can't hold water. I wasn't telling yo ass nothing. You probably told her about this.

Shut up! No I didn't. You did a good job T. Who helped you? I know you didn't do it by yourself!

Nah., You know Ron helped me.

Who?

You know Ronny. Twin?

Oh, yeah, I remember his fine ass. He single?

Yeah. He remembers you too. Yall know how Tiny is though.

She'll be alright.

She always talking about you like you in the room. I swear she been talking about you and how she wanted to come to Miami for your birthday. How you weren't gone do nothing and blah blah.

Shut up but I wasn't doing shit cuz she wasn't there. I'm glad you threw this for her so now we can bring my birthday in together.

Yea don't get beat up. I'm giving y'all a curfew.

Giving us? Nigga you betta be there too.

Imma be there sis. Somebody gotta watch y'all.

"You ain't never met a dope bitch, dope bitch." Sherri looking at Tony.

You know this Me and Tiny shit. Dope Bitch, Dope Bitch!

In walks, Tiny right on que, making her way to Sherri, rapping along as the two girls get caught up in the music. They didn't notice it, but it seemed as if the music was getting louder and louder. "You aint never met a dope bitch, dope bitch like me. Make a nigga snort it up like a whole key." Ahhhhhh yess!!! the girl's scream.

In walks Miami dopest female artist Nisha Blanco.

"Lick on my neck and go down to my breast do you know what is next yes!!!" After performing Nisha gives Ri a Happy Birthday shout out and sat at the table joining the festivities.

Happy Birthday Sis!

Yeah. Happy birthday Ri as Ron hands her a dozen of roses and balloons.

Awe thanks so much y'all! She looks at Tony and you didn't tell me.

Tony laughs. Her ass aint know. I told you y'all can't hold water. All Tiny ass been talking about is you and yo damn birthday. Me and Ron was both sick of hearing it so we came together and put this together for y'all.

Aww thanks y'all.

Oh, shit I almost forgot Happy Birthday Sis! Tiny hands her the box she was just given. Sherri opens it. It's a bracelet that matches with the one he bought Tiny earlier; each diamond for the years the girls been friends and one centered with their birthstone color.

Finishing the night off the girls had to take a million and one pictures repeatedly. Everybody was stumbling to their cars. Rod took Ron's car, Ron took Sherri's car, Antwan took Tony's car, and Tony took Tiny's car.

Everybody was supposed to meet at Tiny's house but only Tony, Tiny, Ron, and Sherri made it there.

Yo! y'all can just crash here. Pick a room. Shit, y'all ah figure it out. Tony said carrying Tiny wasted ass up the stairs. Ron helped Sherri to one of the guest rooms.

Thanks, so much Ron. Ri said slurring.

You welcome, as he helps Sherri into bed.

Lay down,

you laying with me?

 No. You're drunk.

No. I'm grown. Come lay next to me. I ain't gonna bite you.

 Ron laid next to her and cuddled up with her until they both dosed off.

A TEST OF LOYALTY

Shaking uncontrollably, Tiny sits on the end of her best friend's bed. Tiny began to become even more nervous than before; she pulls out her phone and dials the one person she knew she could trust. Tiny knew that this person would be there in a heartbeat, that person was her Best friend Sherri.

Three rings before she answered.

After hello, the only thing Tiny said was, I need you. Fifteen minutes. Your house.

You could hear Sherri talking to her background. Aye y'all I'm sorry. I gotta go, something came up.

Call ended.

Grabbing her keys, she took off to head home.

They had that "No Questions Asked" type of bond, but in person the questions were none stop. Growing up and going through every phase of life together, no one knew them better than one another. They shared a bond so deep that they'll have an entire conversation without words and knew exactly what the other person was thinking.

Ten minutes later, Tiny still stunned and scared, she looks at this backpack in disbelief.

Not only what she had witnessed earlier today but what she had so far left her speechless. Tiny snatches it up and heads out to meet her bestie.

Tiny get into the car.

Girl who the fuck you hiding from? Sherri asks regularly, not noticing the tears coming down her sister's face. Putting the car in reverse, foot still on breaks she demanded, where we going?

My house!

Wait. What the fuck! You were just at home. You cheating bitch? With a malicious look on her face. Yet, Sherri's whole mood changed as soon as she looked over at Tiny. Exchanging a hug and a moment of "bitch what the fuck is going on?" and "it's fucked up without moving a muscle". Tiny pushes the backpack to Sherri.

Open it! Idk what the fuck to do?

Sherri looks inside. Wait a minute bitch. You called me home like u were dying cuz you wanna play chess?

Tiny shot a sharp look at Sherri. Bitch now is not the time for your incompetence.

Pulling the board out the bag, she notices the two ounces of weed. Wait. What the fuck? Who the fuck? Bitch how? Where?

Noticing Tiny was quiet and quite nervous Sherri stopped asking questions and felt inside the bag again. Feeling the wad of cash at the bottom of the bag, she lifts it up without exposing it to the world.

Ok Tee. You scaring me start talking now!!

Tiny busted out in tears. They took them away from me. Both of them. I want them to pay for it. I saw it. I saw it all. I don't have nothing or no one.

Who? Wait don't fuckin tell me? Not. Nooo!!!

Tiny was not responsive. Her face said it all and in that moment. The two broke down.

What am I supposed to do? Where am, I supposed to go from here?

For starters let's get out of here and get somewhere safe. Let's get a room.

The car filled with silence.

I gotta go home and deal with the police and what not.

Wait a minute Tee you didn't?

I didn't have a choice. Had I stayed them mothafuckas would've known I was home that's why I need you to say I been with you at yo house. Act like you don't know shit, you just dropping me off and leaving.

Turning on her block you could see the police lights flashing. Reaching the front of Tiny's house, her entire demeanor changed.

Fucking snake. Why this pussy here?

Girl who? What the fuck is going on Tiny?

Girl my snake of an uncle. This bitch at my house. Was he coming back to finish me off?

Yo uncle. Yo uncle who?

G. Him and two of his homeboys responsible for this.

Omg Tee. No. Calm down. We will handle him. Tell me the details later, but for now, play your role and don't tell the police shit. He gone answer for them fucking tears sis.

I'll call you soon as I'm clear to talk.

Tiny exits the car and tells Ri not to tell Tony and to act like everything is normal when he drops the car off. Tiny walks in, calling out for her parents, noticing the yellow tape. Ma, Daddy, what happened in here?

In walks G. He favored his brother in many ways. Come here baby girl. Have a seat.

Tiny takes a seat on their couch as G lie straight through his teeth. Tiny breaks down crying, remembering she just witnessed this same motherfucker take her parents' lives. Now he was in her face, telling her how he was sorry and everything would be alright. Anger filled Tiny and intruded her thoughts all she could hear was her mom saying *See you in hell* then visualized saying that to her Uncle once he took his last breath.

Where you staying at tonight baby girl? I know you don't wanna stay here. You welcomed to stay at my place.

Tiny thought to herself *the nerve of this motherfucker.* Um, its ok Uncle G. Imma stay at Ri's house. Let me call her and tell her come pick me up.

Ok the police want to ask you a few questions.

After talking to the police Tiny heads up to her room and gathers some of her personal items to take with her. While upstairs, Tiny decided to call an Uber and get a hotel room. She needed the air and space.

Walking down the stairs alright G, I'm gone I'll call you in the morning.

   Alright baby girl your ride here?

Yep! Walking out the front door.

6 a.m.

Gazing at the ceiling, Tiny is interrupted by a knock at the door. Confused, because of the DO NOT DISTURB sign posted on her door. *Who could it be? Who knew where she was located?* She grabs her pistol and inches toward the door. Looking through the peephole she doesn't see anyone. Now she's frantic and pacing back and forth. *Who the fuck is it? I didn't tell anyone. Are they after me? Do they know I got it?*

Bitch I KNOW YOU IN THERE IMMA KILL YOU AND THAT NIGGA! A drunk man's voice shouts, as the unidentified person began banging harder. Cassandra! I swear to God bring yo ass out here now. BOOM! The knocks grew louder taking a deep breath to quickly gather herself.

She was almost instantly interrupted. Another knock at the door startles her; she cocks her pistol as she cracks the door. Who the fuck is it?

Slightly staring out of the crack, with only a chain to separate the two, a startled, young, dark skin, scruffy faced cat shocked at the face behind the door.

Ahh ahh umm. My bad ma I thought you were...

I don't give a fuck who you thought I was. Why the fuck you banging on my got damn door sounding dumb as fuck and loud as fuck for no fucking reason!? I hope he fuckin her brains out you fucking imbecile! Get the fuck away from my door.

She spazzed and slams the door shut! Tiny annoyed and realizing it is now a new day, she checks her phone. She had many missed calls and text messages from Sherri and Tony.

She dials Sherri.

One ring before Ri picked up.

Bitch where the fuck are you? Tony gone kick yo ass if he find you before I do.

I'm at the Marriott downtown come get me.

The Marriott with who? Alright girl I'm on my way.

Ri pulls up and Tiny get in.

Alright I got all the answers you need, but bitch let me tell you what the fuck happened this morning.

So, last night, after dealing with that snake and them pigs, the first place I went nervous and scared was to the hotel.

Tell me why a drunk mothafucka came banging on the door at six o`clock in the morning looking for his Bitch and you know my paranoid ass.

I can only imagine girrllllllllll. What did u do?

Before or after my heart attack? as both the girls chuckle.

I'm thinking the motherfuckas saw me and followed me there. So, I'm pacing back and forth trying to gather my thoughts.

Only thing I could reason was to grab the pistol before I went to the door and shoved it in his face.

Who? Girl what the fuck happened and when did this happen?

Ok let me start from the top. So yesterday when I left school, Daddy was looking for the chess board out in the shed so we could play. You know how he always made us do work and play life games whenever we didn't go to school. Yesterday was no different and, and.

Tiny just started sobbing and weeping.

Sherri, "get it out."

His own brother took his life over five thousand dollars. Ri began comforting her. Then he shot her, he shot her in her face.

The tears coming down both girls face as Tiny describes in detail her parent's gruesome death.

Sherri pulls in front of her house and park. She looks at her best friend in the face. Do you love me?

Like a motherfucking sister!

You wouldn't let anything happen to me, right?

No! RI what the fuck is up you scaring me!?

I love you too and that's exactly how I feel. Somebody gotta answer to them tears Sis. You know who right?

The girls stared at each other briefly.

Tiny spoke first, What's first rule sis?

Loyalty is law. Sherri responds. Second rule?

Tiny rebuttal, we aint seen shit. We aint heard shit so we don't know shit.

The two share a laugh.

Exactly! Let's go in this house and put something on yo stomach. I'm sure Big mama cooked. In walks the two girls and sure enough Big Mama cooked; BBQ beef ribs, macaroni, yams, black eyed peas and cornbread.

Gone in there and wash y'all hands. Tinyesha you know you welcome here anytime baby. Sit right there let me get you a plate. Now Tiny if you gone be staying here tell Sherri scoot on over and get you a key made Ion believe in getting out my bed to open the door for y'all wild kids.

Ok Big Mama I'll let you know soon. I am still taking everything in.

Ok nah you welcome to stay.

Thanks, Big Mama.

The two girls eat, then head down the stairs. Upon entering the room, a mix of black cherry air freshener and marijuana filled the room. Sherri sits on the edge of her bed and pulls out her rolling tray and begins rolling a fat blunt.

I got just what you need to calm yo nerves.

Tiny looks up and snatches the blunt from Ri.

You damn right you do. What the fuck we gone do RI?

Sherri gets up and heads to her closet she pulls the string to turn on her light.

Come in here and pass the got damn blunt rookie.

Tiny makes her way to the closet. I need this more than you. Yo dumb ass should've rolled two.

Snatching the blunt back, Girl whatever! I'll roll another one, but take your pick.

Tiny moving Sherri out the way to get a better view, Bitch what the fuck? Who you at war with?

Admiring the view, but a little concerned. Ri had built an arsenal in the back of her closet. Tiny smiling and grabs one of her best-friend pistols.

Ooh this one is pretty and manageable.

Is that the one you want?

Yep this one!

What the fuck you gone do with it? Ri asks Tiny cocks it back, "use it."

Sherri seeing the spark in Tiny's eye made her proud.

Tee I heard he back on that shit and he'll be round P house around midnight tonight to get his fix. That'll be perfect; catch him in the ally, No witnesses, No investigating.

No Turning Back

1 a.m.

G rolls over and calls his order in. Scratching his beard, walking in the living room and asking Troy to take him over to P crib so he can get his daily fix. Troy was hesitant at first, telling him to go alone but knowing his drunk ass was in no condition to drive.

Get up nigga.

Alright nigga. Shit, but I just ordered me some Coney so I'm stopping and getting my food first. Ole itching ass nigga.

The two head out and first stopped at Coney Island as promised by Troy.

It's 99cent Coney day I had to get my fix. Troy said, talking shit to G.

G dismisses him. Man, come yo fat ass on.

As Troy takes a bite of his Coney dog he dropped chili on his pants due to rushing. He pulls off and makes his way towards P crib.

2am

Small talk and the smell of Mary J filled the air of Sherri black grand am. "Lord knows I opposed dropping O's but money woes and pressure from bill collectors--," 3D Na'tee Wake Me up played over the car speakers.

Who is that Tiny asked?

One of the hottest chicks to ever touch a mic, you feeling that shit aint you? Ri shot back, "I know you can relate" Just listen to the words and metaphors and how they fit so perfectly together.

Here yo ass go with this music science pass the got damn blunt Tiny says as she listened to Sherri carry on about how many more songs she'd love and relate to and how raw this artist was. Tiny did relate and got lost in the music as it triggered quite a few memories.

Sherri realizes Tiny is now zoned out she asked, "are you ready to share the details?" Tiny still staring off into space shared every intricate detail of her uncle killing her parents and how he had told her mama she better be glad that Tiny was at school cuz he would've killed her too. Anger grew deeper and deeper inside Sherri. "This motherfucka need to hurry up so he can die." Tiny snaps out of her zone and looks at Sherri as if she said something foreign.

Tinyesha Marie Jones for the last time are you sure you ready for this? Cuz if not we can go home now.

That motherfucker gotta pay Ri. He killed them both and had the fuckin nerves to hug me in my parents' house and invited me to stay with him. I'm not a killer you know that but I can't live knowing what he did and he walking around like shit cool.

OK now just know when we get out of this car ain't no turning back.

2:30 a.m.

Where these motherfuckas at? Ri asked growing more impatient by the second. Then the all black Camaro pulled up and hits the lights.

Show time! Sherri said as they got out the car.

Walking down the alley, stumbling laughing, Tiny falls over Sherri. She kneels.

Bitch see this why I don't drink with you. Get the fuck up.

Troy yells out to G.

Yo check these hoes out.

G looks off and sees the girls and decides to walk up. Troy walks right behind him.

Aye are y'all ok?

Getting closer and closer G realizes it's his niece Tinyesha.

What the fuck you doing out here like this?

Fuck you! Tiny shouts as she rises to her feet

Ri instantly let three shots rang leaving Troy lifeless. With the pistol to his face stuttering.

Whhhat whaatt you doing baby girl? Put the gun down. What's wrong with you Tiny?

Shut the fuck up pussy! I saw everything!

What the fuck you talking about Tinyesha?

I was home from school, so I guess you forgot to do me first, right?

G began laughing hysterically this sends Tiny into a rage.

Tell my mother hello for me.

She pulled the trigger.

Sherri starts rushing over to Tiny and grabs the pistol from her hands.

Damn Sis can't lie. I aint think you had it in you.

Please Ri, never make me relive this again.

To the grave baby. To the grave.

The two rode home in complete silence passing the Dutch back and forth.

I love you sister.

I love you too.

The girls shared that moment before going in.

Ulterior Motives

A scruffy yet slurring voice could be heard from the entrance of this old ran down apartment on Detroit's west side. The outside looked just how the inside smelled, awful. Walking down this long hallway was creepy. It was dark and the floors creaked like the place hadn't been renovated in years. A mixture of booze, ass, old trash and marijuana filled the air. Standing a few feet away, she could finally make out what was being said before entering.

Fuck them they walk around like the perfect couple but I know something. Neither of them know about each other that'll ruin their power couple charades! That's posed to be my bitch and my life. And this hoe ass nigga posed to be my brother. Let his Master get him wrapped up in this bullshit. Fuck him too!

As he is pacing back and forth with nothing but his boxers on, pistol in one hand 40 oz. in other. Sandy walks in.

What you in here ranting about now? What the fuck, look at you, it's only noon and you wasted already?

He tosses her up against the wall with his hands around her neck.

Bitch don't come up in here and disrespect me. These shiesty motherfuckas been playing me this whole time and I want everything they hid from me. Fuck them niggas! I plan on fucking that bitch too, but in the meantime. Imma fuck you.

He slides his boxers down, lifts her dress, and went to work. Pounding her the entire time spurting out parts of his envious plan to take what he felt belonged to him. *That's his money his woman and his life.* After five minutes, he was fast asleep.

Sandy sitting up coming up with a plan of her own. Once her need for him had dissolved so would the entire relationship. She knew he didn't have a chance with Tiny, especially after watching her in action. Seeing Tiny turned her on. *Ion see how he maintain his composure though. Being that close, that often, and not folding instantly.* She reverted to her own plan. *Tony would be mine even if only for one night.* She picks up her partner's phone and searched for T's contact.

Yo T meet me at the Car Wash. I need to rap with you bout some shit.

Alright give me thirty minutes I'll be there.

Sandy deleted the message out of the phone. Memorizing the number, she put the phone back and slipped out the house to meet T at the Car Wash.

Tiny and Tony had spent the day in enjoying each other's company when T received a message from Rod to meet him at the car wash. T gets up and heads for the door.

 I'll be back baby. Give me kiss.

Where you going?

I gotta go meet Rod at the car wash. I shouldn't be long. You want some food while I'm out? Never mind, yo fat ass always down to eat. Imma stop at the crab house.

Ok babe.

Tiny kisses him and watch from the front window as he pulls off. She calls Ri.

Get here now! Drive by time

Ri pulls up.

What's up Tee? Who we sliding on?

I think Tony cheating again. He been acting real fucking weird. He got a text and ran out the door today. Talking bout, it's from Rod. So, I'm bout go see cuz them niggas aint that close.

Ok where we going?

The Car Wash.

On Joy Rd?

No. On 7mile.

Sherri hits South field freeway and head up there.

Tony pulls in the Car Wash. He directs his car up to a vacuum. Getting out, he sees a few familiar cars, but he couldn't spot Rod or Ron. A familiar voice calls out.

What's up T? As she walks up to his car.

Wassup loon? What you doing up here?

Shit you if you let me?

There you go what's wrong with you?

Sandy leans in grabs his hands and places them on her butt. She starts whispering in his ear.

Don't act like you don't want this.

Tony smiling. I don't.

Tiny and Ri pulls up. Tiny jumps right out.

I fucking knew it.

She swings and drops Sandy with one hit. She lands a few more licks before Tony grabs her.

Baby, it's not what you think calm down. I came here to meet Rod.

Calm down?

Tiny starts fighting and cursing at him. You let this bitch come to my place of business too and stir up some shit?

He puts her in the car while she's still going off on him. Meanwhile Ri jumped out to finish off what Tiny started.

Sis nooo. Get yo ass in the car! Why the fuck you bring her up here for this shit anyway?

Sandy laid out, beat up and bloodied.

You and the whole fucking city know how I get down. Why the fuck you put me in this situation? I swear I'm done with you this time. You aint shit I swear!!!

Tony pulling his phone out; he shows Tiny the text he got.

You still don't fucking trust me? I didn't come here to meet no fucking body, but Rod.

Whatever nigga let me see yo phone!

She called the number he received his text from and it began ringing on Sandy. Tony, now confused, gets silent and pulls off making sure Sherri left too.

Sandy sent him a text. **I'm sorry I didn't mean to get us caught, but I love you. Please don't leave me Tony**.

What the fuck is this? I don't believe you lying bitch. I hate you.

Really? I'm trying to understand what the fuck just happened.

Exactly! Dumb ass take me home and get the fuck on. Hope that bitch can house you.

After dropping Tiny off, Tony kept calling Ron but couldn't get him on the phone. He went to his little brother house to chill out.

Rod wakes up and head to Antwan's house. He walks in on Tony telling the story.

Instantly feeling betrayed. He came up with a plan of his own that would work out in his favor because neither of the two knew what he knew. Rod had to play his cards right to make sure his hands stayed cleaned.

Tiny calls Vee and asks her if she could run the shop for a while because she needed some time to clear her mind after what happened. She told Vee the story.

I knew it was something that wasn't right with that girl. But alright Tee. I got you.

No Wool Over My Eyes

August 13th

Nina calls Sandy and asked if she could take her to work. Letting her know Tiny still hadn't been back. Sandy agreed.

Nina got out the car and Vee instantly recognized the car but decided to play it cool.

That's yo new boo? Girl no that's my best friend. My car in the shop so I had to get it dropped off today.

Oh, ok just being me nosey. You know.

Yeah, I know.

Rod hands Ron his spare keys.

I need you to go get that for me. Imma be a minute before I get there. Leave the door open I got this lil freak coming over.

Yeah alright you better strap up fucking these nasty hoes.

Rod dismissed him and kept it pushing.

Vee closed the shop around eight and decided to get some Bread Basket before heading in. But soon as she hit the freeway, she noticed that same 300 who belonged to this mystery girl. The private investigator clicked into Vee so she decided to follow.

Taking the 8mile exit, Vee knew exactly where she was going but was really hoping she was wrong.

They turned left on the first street, three houses down the second block is where Rod lived. Vee parked at the corner of the first street and killed her lights.

She watched Sandy go in the house and what appeared to be Rod come. It wasn't until the car rode past and she got a clear view. *OMG Ron? What the fuck?* Vee began scratching her head trying to figure it all out. *This messier than I thought but why though?* Then it dawned on her *they gotta know about Tiny side businesses and been plotting on robbing her. I gotta warn her and Tony.*

Ron did just what his brother asked him to do. Go home, get his dope, and put it up for him. He did this right before heading out for a night on the town with his new-found lady.

Vee began blowing up Tiny's phone but Tiny wasn't accepting calls from anyone except Sherri. She finally got Tony to answer the phone and told him everything. Tony pulled up, slid in Rod crib while Sandy was in the shower. He snuck in and snatched the shower curtain back.

Bitch you thought I was dumb?

Tony grabs her by the throat before slamming her head in to the wall. Sandy falling to floor Tony began kicking her in her stomach.

Bitch! I just lost everything cuz of you! Now my own motherfucking brother tried to set me up. Fuck that nigga too. Bitch I should off you.

Tony grabs some sheets and ties Sandy up but not before carving the letter RD into her face. Vee came to assist by helping put her in trunk.

Thanks, Vee. I'll take it from here.

What we gone do about her best friend?

I don't know yet but still go to shop in the morning and run everything normal alright?

Alright. Be careful T.

You too. Thanks again Vee. I got you for this one.

They both head in. Still trying to reach Tiny, neither of them was successful. Tony began blowing up Sherri phone but her voicemail kept picking up. Sherri wakes up around 7a.m. after enjoying her long night. She checks her messages and began responding. She calls Tiny and tell her something is wrong and that she need to speak with Tony. Tiny wasn't trying to hear it though.

Bitch was you not there? Fuck that nigga for real this time.

Well I feel that but call that nigga. He sounded spooked on my voicemail.

Voicemail?

Oh, yea it better be a real problem.

Lies Hurt Worse Than the Truth

August 14, 91 degrees 9 a.m.

Birds chirping, bees buzzing, the sun beaming down, with no wind in sight.

Tiny calls T back.

Tony immediately states, we got a problem and I need you.

 NO FUCK YOU! You got a problem.

But Tinyesha Marie Jackson I need you! Let's fix this.

IF YOU KEEP YO DICK IN YO PANTS, WE WOULDN'T HAVE TO FIX SHIT!

Tiny abruptly ends the call, she tosses her phone in the passenger seat as she slams the door to her bright yellow Camaro. She sped off and headed to her salon. Her thoughts racing back and forth. *What the fuck wrong with this nigga? Do he think I'm stupid? But I can't leave him to dry like that. He fucked up this time. Oooh stupid ass!* She shouts.

She reaches her salon with pain, anxiety and anger clouding her judgment and vision because she failed to see Rod's black Impala parked on the side of Paradise. Jumping out, Tiny runs to her back office, opens her safe, and removed an envelope.

Vee tried to get a word in but failed drastically. Dialing her best friend's number as she jumps back in her car and heads where she swore up and down she wasn't going.

Who you with? Where you at? Can you meet me?

Sherri hits her with a million questions. Where you at? Are you OK? Are you being followed?

Bitch, why the fuck you sound so got damn paranoid? What you doing you aint got no business? Or should I say who?

You know me, don't you?

The girls chuckle.

Nah. I need you to come meet me. We talked and he is sounding all weird talking about meet him and I got a weird feeling about it. You know we aint been talking since I caught him with the community pussy.

Damn I need to know that yo head is clear Tee. I aint trying to bail you out.

I'm good but why you aint left out yet?

I was a little tied up!

I need you. I don't care who you fucking. I am nervous RI.

OK make sure you're not being followed and promise you not gone be mad at me!

Girl you high? Paranoid ass I should be the paranoid one.

I don't know what the fuck is wrong with this nigga I catch him with this hoe. Now he thinks I'm supposed to just come running because he said so?

RI laughs. Aint that what you doing though? But for real Tee. --OK I promise! -- I'm heading out now.

Sherri looks over to this brown skin, handsome, clean cut brother.

Can you ride with me?

I don't know what the fuck is going on?!

So, focused on the conversation Tiny never saw the black Impala or grey Taurus. A few cars behind the Black Impala made every turn and took every exit she did. Tiny was definitely off her game. She would've usually been picked up on her being followed.

The Grey Taurus saw the Camaro slowing down and decided to ride past. The impala, on the other hand, stopped and parked just perfect enough to see and not be seen. Tiny pulls up, parks in a secluded area, and takes a deep breath. Then she took a few looks around. All she could see were trees.

Message to RI. **Bitch I got a funny feeling get here quick.** Message sent.

Tony walks up and gets in the car. Were you followed?

Fuck you!

Tiny, now isn't the time for this. Were you followed?

No dumb ass. What the fuck?

He snatches her phone and turns it off. Get out of the car and shut the fuck up.

Tony led her down this trail in the middle of what appeared to be an area of woods. Getting closer and closer Tiny stops and asked: Are you trying to kill me? Because it's other ways we can settle this.

Tony looks at her with pain in his eyes. Are you serious? You think I'd hurt you? That's so low of you. He stated while reaching his destination. This! This! is what the fuck I've been doing. I wasn't fucking this bitch.

I been trying to figure out who her inside man was and I think I have a damn good idea. That hoe ass nigga Ron supposed to be my fucking brother. Vee saw everything so I went and got her from Rod house last night. Those motherfuckers have been plotting on us. I swear baby I didn't fuck this girl. Ever! She was stalking me at the gym. I never knew she came to the shop.

Tiny spits on Sandy and kicks her in the mouth causing her to lose her front teeth. You fucked with the right one at the wrong time bitch!

A pair of Footsteps could be heard crunching on the leaves as two people could be heard in distance.

Ron though? How did you turn him? I never would've fucking thought. That's like my little brother. Both of y'all will pay.

Sherri walks up in the opposite direction from where Tiny and Tony came. She was happy at the sight but unhappy at the story. Wait what happened? And when?

Where the fuck you come from? I thought you said you weren't followed Tiny!

Tiny responded rolling her eyes at him.

Tony hissed. Ron hoe ass crossed me for a bitch. I never thought in a million years.

Sherri now extremely confused as Ron walks up from behind her. I did what nigga? And with who?

Tony draws his pistol and points it at Ron. You hoe ass nigga. Vee saw you leaving from being with this bitch last night!

Wait bro, you sure? cuz we were together the whole night.

Tiny side eyes Ri.

Sherri pouts. Bitch I told you don't be mad. Shit.

But y'all gotta have it all wrong.

Yeah brother you do.

Ron drew his pistol. Have you ever had to question me? What the fuck changed now? Some street talk? I thought I was yo fucking brother. This aint what brothers do my nigga.

With pistols drawn and the two girls trying to make light of the situation, let's go over this again. Are you sure it was Ron?

That's who I got the fucking messages from and everything. It gotta be this nigga!

Messages? Nigga, what the fuck you talking about?

Yo lil bitch texted me to meet you at the car wash. This is how all this shit went left.

Wait. Nigga, what? I don't even know this bitch. You sure that was me and not Rod?

Dawning on everybody it could be mistaken identity. The boys lowered their guns and concluded there was no other valid explanation but Rod.

Let's get out of here. What we gone do with her? Sherri asks.

Whatever you want sis!

Ri snatches the pistol from Ron takes one look at Tiny. Tiny had the same scared look on her face ten years earlier without wasting another second Sherri puts one in Sandy head.

Loyalty is law. Sherri sneered.

Sherri handed Ron his gun back; the couples head to their cars neither of them noticing the trail behind them. They dart to Tiny and Tony's house. The guys take the girls car and the girls rode together in Tony's truck.

I told you sis I always got yo back. Sherri stated.

Tiny cuts her phone back on. A block away from the house Tiny receives a message from Vee.

I think I fucked up. It wasn't Ron it was Rod and he's been following you since he left the shop. I'm behind him. Be careful.

Before Tiny could react. *SCCCCRRRHHHH*

The screeching of tires and the bending of metal could be heard blocks over.

Rod smacked his car in the back of Tees truck. Sending the truck flipping Tony and Ron take off on feet reaching the scene. They notice the Black Impala first, this sends Tony over the top. He draws his pistol and heads over to Rod

Im killing this hoe ass nigga.

Nah I can't let you do that Ron said. loyalty is law. Blood for blood.

Well you gotta do what you gone do little brother loyalty is law and he crossed the line.

Rod lets off few rounds as Ron & T both take cover. Bullets rang out from every which way ten minutes before all fire ceased Ron steps out from behind the tree.

Put the guns down man what the fuck?

Fuck that nigga he gotta die now. As T fired his last round through Rods car.

You empty now huh pussy? Rod spats. Making his way to his feet.

Tony peeking from behind his truck. Yea OK nigga come see.

Ron comes from behind a tree now standing between Rod and Tony cars. Tony rise to his feet and heads towards Rod. Rod makes his way out of his impala with a bloodied lip.

Put a bullet in this nigga Ron. *He got everything but don't want to share shit think giving me a job with his bitch was enough of the pie. I know about his little apartment on the east side too. Did he tell you about That little side business? You following this nigga round and he playing you. Yea nigga you thought you was so low-key, love the gym underplay too.*

T amused because Rod still didn't have shit on him that Ron didn't know and the site of him pleading made it even sweeter.

Nigga I should've killed you when my bitch told me to Tony spits back at Rod.

That's our bitch nigga! Ron!! Rod yells out, man We can have it all. He don't do shit for us anyway. The fuck you waiting on? Angered that his brother could be this envious and spiteful.

Ron interrupts man yall both my fucking brothers and yall at war when we can all win and build an empire. you did this shit over some money? You not fucking broke the fuck man? The fuck is wrong with you.?

Rod spits blood in Ron face blood, right? Fuck you nigga you ain't no brother of mine. You just look like me. Keep letting this pussy play you.

You know what you right fuck you. Blood for blood. You always wanted to be me.

As Ron wipes the spit from his eyes and pulled the trigger. The two men standing rush back to the truck where they women were. Disgusted at the sight and wanting to get away from the scene they started pulling them out of the car.

Vee walks up, Yall might wanna get the fuck on, I'll explain later but for now I got them.

The two men takes her advice and agreed that it'd be best if they left and met them at the hospital. The sirens from the ambulance could be heard in distance. They ran back to the house Ron tossed the guns in Sherri's car and grabbed two hoodies for him and T. As T started Tiny car and headed up to the hospital. Ron jumps in the passenger seat wiping his sweaty hands on his pants. We gotta do something about these bodies bro, yea but you Know the hook all over it now T responds as they approach A red light.

Ron grabs the manila envelope in the middle of the car and asks T bro you slipping like this? As he opens it and is shocked by the contents. Yo bro the fuck is this? As he turns to T. Bro, Bro? the fuck man is you high? still no response! Ron taps T and his body is limp. Jumping out Ron runs to the driver door and pushes T over to the passenger side. When the fuck, this happen looking at the blood on his hands. I can't lose you too man not today not like this. Ron knowing to avoid hospitals at all costs he called the one person who would help them.

Ahh this shit hurt! Looking around, and seeing all these cords I instantly recognized where I was. Nurse, Nurse, somebody, come tell me what the fuck is going on. Nurseeee.

Hello Mrs. Dennis calm down you were involved in an auto accident that seemingly turned violent. You're lucky to be alive. You have a lot of bumps and bruises. Do you recall anything?

Mrs. Dennis? I was in the car talking to my sister and next thing I know I'm here. Wait Tiny, Tiny, where is my sister?

Calm down do you recall anything else?

Bitch where the fuck is my sister? Don't tell me to calm down anymore.
Ma'am we are just trying to figure out--

If you don't answer me about my sister, you gone be trying figure out what happened to you next. Where the fuck is my sister?

Attempting to get up. The pain shot from my toes to my waist. Ahhh. What the fuck?

I'm sorry I didn't mean to upset you. Wait a second you can't get up I will help you. Bringing over a wheelchair.

Wait nurse, help me remember. Why do I need a wheelchair?

Well you have a broken leg, fractured ribs, A gunshot wound, and many cuts and burns.

Gun shot? Who the fuck was shooting?

We were hoping you could tell us.

Can you take me to my sister please? This is too much for me.

Yes, she's back from surgery.

Surgery? What?

When we got inside the room Tiny was sleeping, I waited about 2 hours before she woke up. All we could do was hug each other and let the tears flow.

Bitch don't ever scare me like that again.

Tiny could barely talk but managed to get out Tony.

I searched for her phone and dialed both him and Ron. All my calls going unanswered made my anxiety go through the roof!

Mrs. Jackson? I'm Dr. Topanga how are you feeling? I'm ok my mouth a little dry. What's going on? I'm having trouble recalling.

Jackson? Dennis? Who signed our paperwork?

You have a broken arm and you had to have surgery to have the bullet removed from your stomach. Any idea how that got there?

With a look of confusion, bullet? But I was in a car accident. Yes, you were and lucky to live you lost a lot of blood. Sorry we couldn't save both of you.

Both of us? What you talking about?

With all the blood, you lost we weren't able to save your baby.

Baby? Huh baby? What? When? How long? No God what the fuck?

How far along was she?

About 16weeks.

16 weeks? My baby didn't have a chance at all.

It became a tsunami of tears questions and curses shared between both of us. The pit at the bottom of my stomach turned.

Somebody gotta answer for this shit--

Ring, ring. **Incoming Call from Ron**

Hello? Yall alright

I am but He fucked up right now

How are yall? Fucked up but we breathing.

Ok cool well Tiny will know where we are just tell her 6.

OK! We should be out of here in the next few days see you then.
Ri, I love you! Tell sis I love her too. See yall soon.

STAY TUNED

WHAT LIES AHEAD ? PART 2

COMING SOON!